Synapse

Brendan Hawthorne

TenebrousTexts

Sydney, so his birth certificate says, is 93 years of age yet is mercurial in appearance.

Today he is found sitting in an armchair at a private care home that befits his wealth and conditions of mind. He has a regular visitor who sits next to him listening to his memories as he recants them in no particular order.

His visitor seems to find him a subject of great personal interest yet no one outside of their relationship knows why.

Sydney is prone to ramble in thought.

As his mind wanders he interlaces fact with fiction and absorbs distant conversations that he latches onto in passing.

This book, written and conceived by Brendan Hawthorne and illustrated by artist Jason Fullwood, represents the final confessions of a man seeking clarity of mind.

Is he bragging about his dealings in life or simply cleansing his earthbound soul before his next incarnation?

That, dear reader, is for you to determine.

Through One Way Glass

It is there in these dark days of incarceration that I meet them all once again. The same ghosts who project themselves into my mind even now to this minute. Those guilty victims of circumstance parade their fears and victories in a glitz-posed gloomy collective past.

I am at a railroad crossroad junction bathed in glaring lights and surrounded by deafening blaring horns.

A fanfare is ringing out for all painted butterflies and grotesque shadows that still eat away at the cortex of my remembrances.

Would you like a cup of tea?

Yes please.

One sugar?

That's right, thank you.

1 Dead Speak

Can you hear it?
Listen!
There!
Just then.
Did you miss it?
Surely you heard it?
There!
Just as the horse drawn hearse approaches in silence.
Yes!
Maria is here again.
I can hear her.
The sound of fingernails thickened with death scraping
at freedom.
Those armour-plated claw hooks capping knuckle-bound
fingers ingrained with splinters of fine English oak.
There she is free to roam the bounds of headstones.
She is as fleeting as a midnight kiss.
As transient as a spring time storm.
Her perfume drifts,
Heady as summer
Heavy as violets laced with coffin varnish and deck tar.
Bless her.
Her soul was lost so long since ...
Shhhh!
Listen!
Ah there she is.
Over there.
A lone mourner seeking her love again tonight.

Church clock chimes the anniversary of departure as gravediggers smoke snips from clay pipes.

They lean on their shovels and spit.

Spit as only regular smokers do.

They swear that their job will be the death of them as they whistle wheeze a laugh through missing teeth.

And so what of Maria?

Maria's only love was a daughter of the Spanish Main.

Eleanore, oh Eleanore, such a wild and untamed soul.

Many called her name but she was only ever faithful to one.

She sailed on many a man-o'-war.

And sank many a man in port beneath a drinks table to lighten his purse under the white flag of Libertaria.

She knew the value of true freedom.

Her hair rat-tailed the seven winds in full sail on high seas.

She stood prow proud at the head of her fleet.

Directing broadside cannons across flashing cutlasses.

The treasures will be all hers for now.

For a percentage at port this peasant girl had become Queen of the Seas.

Politics inevitably changed with the fickle nature of monarchs and councils and, for all she had done in the name of her country, she was outlawed when allies became enemies of the state and freebooters became inconsequential rogues awaiting the crossroad gibbet.

She was never once beleaguered nor held in the doldrums of life until that is…

Eleanore had one safe port left at her disposal. An island retreat with a crew that would follow her to the ends of the earth and, in time, to the end of a rope if lead or steel didn't take them first.

She was a lover many times over, but only ever loved once.

Her true love was always to be Maria.

Maria's husband was a man of politics and lacked any humility and diplomacy.

He was violent towards Maria so much so that she carried his scars of brutality both externally and internally.

At a state function Maria saw the beauty and freedom of Eleanore.

To her, she was everything she wanted a lover to be.

Eleanore saw the sadness in Maria's eyes and soon they found tenderness in the boudoir abandonment of each other's arms.

Tropical heat seared through their minds and bodies, their sweat intermingling in rapture just before the door burst in on them on that tempestuous night.

Maria's throat was cut by her enraged husband.

Her life blood flowed through Eleanore's fingers as she tried to stem the wave of blood that engulfed a look of sheer horror.

Her blood pooled on the floor forming the seeping shapes of red roses.

Eleanore was beaten unconscious and transported to a labour camp on the island and, after many nights of torture by Maria's husband, she was locked in a cargo chest for hours on end.

She was brought out into the dim light and fed on sickening scraps before the nightmares would inevitably begin again.

For days and nights she endured what had become of her existence, before finally succumbing to the ravages of her tormentor.

She never made the punishing journey from the West Indies to the mines of Africa.

Barely a breath left in her body, she was simply weighted and ditched overboard from the deck of a trades winds clipper.

She hit the waves somewhere in the mid-Atlantic.

The only thing Eleanore's disturbed soul required was to be given its rest from the rolling seas by being placed in home soil.

On a particular full moon and accompanying high tide her funeral is prepared here in this cemetery close to the sea.

Some say there is one funeral for every day she spent in captivity.

There is always one mourner, a lady dressed in deepest black with a scarf about her neck, wearing a hint of violet perfume.

You might just hear Maria whisper 'Eleanore' as she calls to the winds of a turning tide waiting for her beloved to return.

Upon that single moment of meeting their souls are seen to entwine in a lingering embrace and a passionate kiss. Red rose petals confetti-shower down upon the blank headstone, awaiting two names from the stonemason's chisel.

Etched in eternity Eleanore sighs knowing she can rest her head once more upon the bosoms of both her lover and the shores of home.

They are here again, this night.

Listen.

For no weight of soil, flow of tide nor time and distance will ever keep them apart until that final day of rest is bestowed upon them to sleep in eternal peace.

Do you have a piece of Battenberg without the marzipan?

2 Ram Raid

Wiper blades carve swathes across onslaughts of rain bejewelling headlight projections of passing cars. Frictionless edges of carbonised rubber slice through crimson rivers and out to beyond the crackled bullet holed glass that slides beneath them.

A pedestrian hits the bumper like a mosquito. Gets casually catapulted over the roof of a speeding car. Who it was didn't matter to the driver. Only the ram raid did. Dashboard warning lights were blinking like road weary eyes and punched out dials were still recording the last impact in time, date and speed. Steam rose in blistered plumes and hissed through the barred teeth of a twisted radiator grille as split hoses exuded their elixir of stench and vulnerability to a fire storm night.

Tyres squealed in banshee wails, returning calls to sirens and two tones in question and answer blues calls. Xenon beacons punctuated the darkness in rapid fire searings. They were siblings to the sound of popping automatic plasma pulse gun fire, as whitewalls hugged the road in a death grip last stand.

The robbery occurred at 20:52. That's what the digital clock said above the jewellers when drone CCTV began recording the vehicle being driven through the front of the shop. Sixty seconds later diamonds were sparkling on the backseat, resembling stars cast in haste against a night sky. Reversing, the black Ford Ibex careened into a narrow side street crammed with whorehouses and neon lit opium cafes where customers chased speedballs across eastern floor tiles.

There she stands. Waiting for a ride from anyone who could get her away from pimps and drug runners. The car screeches to a halt and the gull wing door rises to beckon her in.

She takes little notice of the driver as he powers through seamless gear changes. She looks through the side window leaving her life behind her in a blurred vision of the past. The driver takes a look at the hiker. He notices the mini skirt that barely covers her panty line, her stockings are laddered and her thin top reveals firm, pert breasts clinging to the curve of fabric. Her lips glisten blood and lip gloss and her eyes are still swollen from a client blow. She feels his gaze sweep across her as he scans each contour in turn. He notices the clutch bag that she holds tightly to her body, no doubt stuffed with the royalties of her trade. He turns his gaze to the rear-view mirror. He has lost the law for now, as his mind turns to a clean bed and the touch of a woman. He has driven for hours, mile on mile of death and holds his life very much on the edge.

"Any motels around here?" he says, tearing through the silence, his parched lips crack like dried up river beds. "We need a new car and somewhere to rest."

She returns from her trance and orders him to "take the next right. There's a lay-by along there. You should be able to change cars. There are pleasure seekers in the woods. They won't want to give away their identities or whereabouts to the law, so your car won't be found or the new one reported missing."

He nods and follows her directions and reasoning.

On reaching the lay-by the doors lift and both driver and passenger alight from the vehicle. She straightens her clothes as he gathers up the diamonds and transfers them to a four litre jeep that someone has hurriedly left on the promise of an intimate liaison. The keys swing in the ignition. He pours petrol from a can over the ram raid Ibex and torches it. The fireball recedes into the darkened mirrors of evening. Ten miles later they turn off the highway into a motel and park up around the back. They pay in advance to reduce suspicion, collecting their towels to set about getting cleaned up. In the wash stand mirror he watches her undress and for a moment he thought that she resembles a lupine being, a predator hunting alone. He puts that thought to one side and passes it off as a trick of the shadows and an absence of light. He knew his imagination was motorheading on uppers and usually this caused him to experience hallucinations and paranoia.

She sits next to him on the bed. She is draped in nothing more than a bath towel. Fresh from the shower she drips in crystal beads. He reaches out and notices a look in her eyes that chills him to the core. He has met and worked for cold-hearted killers in the past, but has never seen this glacial stare before.

The sun rises and casts light across the bed linen that has seen the struggle. She finally decides to get up and go to the bathroom. He lies still. His eyes as wide open as the cut across his throat. Blood congealing into memory. She wipes the switchblade and conceals it once again in her clutch bag. She dresses and picks up the diamonds, looking back at the feast she had to leave behind. One leg of her victim stripped of flesh and an arm missing. To have left him whole would have been criminal. She wipes her mouth and, smiles, she climbs into the waiting jeep after posting the room keys through the night box.

She drives away slowly to avoid any motel curtains twitching before flooring the accelerator, hitting the open freeway in search of another life to take and relieve them of their ill-gotten gains. She howls to the wind and disappears over the horizon as Zevon plays Werewolves on the 8-track. Eleanore smiles to her satiated self and sings 'awooh!'

They are all so very nice here. Could you change channel on the TV for me please?

3 Death's Dog

Some said the form resembled a bear, others a strange hog dog-like creature. All encounters however reported on the stench. Those whose fate dictated their paths crossing could never talk about the effects of looking into those furnace eyes that scanned like laser night sights.

Always after a battle soldiers spoke of this creature that broke into their fevered dreams. The Death Dog haunted their fragile minds. Imprisoned in their skulls, he paced between the hours of three and four. Many a pocket watch fob was turned and checked on awakening in the infirmary when terror struck at this realisation. Some wondered why he snarled his way through a soldier's subconsciousness, especially when the soldier was wounded or on the eve of battle engagement.

A dog of similar description was regularly seen walking across the skulls of many a dead man.

I digress.

An old farmer related this story to me after finding a diary that had been left close to a barbed wire fence after war fell uneasily into peace. The entry in question started in the trenches by a Sgt. O. S. Collins. He remembered going over the top to the trench pusher's whistle and finding himself in a crater in No Man's Land. He realised that his left arm was missing just below the elbow. He could see the dismembered limb a few yards away from where he lay and was still holding the rifle he had set out with moments earlier. The battle roar seemed to diminish when he saw Death's Dog enter the crater and sniff the trail of blood towards him. All pain and suffering ceased in the dog's presence. It was the winter of 1917 and he remembered the dog's eyes shining like carbide torches through the smoke of artillery cross fire. The young Sergeant tried to move but couldn't through fear and trauma. The dog gently lay next to him and they both slept in each others company and shelter.

Owen Collins woke with a start to summer sunshine warming his face and the smell of roses entering his lungs. He was dressed in his favourite tweed trousers and old brown boots, the sleeves of his collarless shirt rolled up to just below the elbows. For a moment he wondered what had happened to the war. It seemed a distant memory. The fields were green and ripening gold and the hum of bullets had been exchanged for the buzz of insects. A dog barked and ran across the fields gambolling in play. Owen could hear his name being called by a familiar and comforting voice. He couldn't believe his ears or his eyes when she came into view. It was Maria, the girl he would have married if it hadn't have been for the war. He looked at the wedding band on his finger and stood up slowly and gathering his senses he ran to her. They caught each other in a long embrace that felt like an eternity.

"Come on lazy bones! The work won't get done with you sleeping the day away. The cottage roof still needs repairing and they've forecast another storm like the one last night. Neighbours said it was a lightning bolt that struck us. They saw it. What were you doing out in all that thunder and lightning? I think that falling branch has done something to your head. Do you remember? It fell from the old oak and knocked you out cold."

Owen looked and felt confused. He looked at both his hands and counted his fingers. They were all present and correct. "Of course I remember. How could I forget? This headache won't let me forget, or this lump." Owen felt the swelling on the back of his head. "I'd better get on with the roof, then," he continued and smiled at the most beautiful lady he had ever seen. He followed Maria into the kitchen of the cottage and picked up a newspaper from the table. The date read 14th July 1919.

"The roof won't get done with you reading a newspaper! That war spoiled you." Owen laughed and went outside, still confused, and set about fixing the storm damaged roof. With a jolt, Owen collected memories like a film on fast forward. He witnessed and felt an onslaught of emotions, reliving the twenty-odd gloriously happy years he and Maria shared until the papers recalled the spring of 1939.

Owen was out walking and thought he saw the ghost of Death's Dog prowling a few paces behind him. Then he heard the town's air raid siren wail its primal cry into the air. An enemy fighter plane swooped in like a bird of prey and before he or the dog could run, the ground was strafed with rapid machine gun fire. Sgt. O. S. Collins fell to the smell of war and the familiar pain of gunshot and shrapnel wounds. He crashed to the floor with a sickening thud, clutching his left arm. As he opened his eyes, Death's Dog stood over him back in that bloody trench of 1917 before drifting into endless sleep. With a whimper and a flash of light, Death's Dog turned into an angel that gently lifted the dead body of Owen Collins high above the battlefield and off into tranquil silence. Sgt. O. S. Collins heard Maria calling him after the all clear had sounded, but it was too late. His soul had flown to a world free from pain where he must wait for Maria to join him in her own time. The dog was never seen again. But an angel did appear in the last days of that Great War and gave comfort to the dying before they fell, in turn, into their own eternal and peaceful sleep.

Have you noticed that the nights are drawing in a bit now?

Maybe it's my eyes going dim.

4 Wailing Blue Moon

Chequerboard streets are stagestruck by the sound of jazz and blues being played in alternating squares. Stepping stone shades of light and tones of dark present Burlesque night clubs rammed with punters seeking a glimpse of sweating flesh served over ice cold gin-based Martinis.

Do you see the compere? Ha ha. He's as cheeky as Pan he is.

Look! The air is filling with cigarette smoke again mixing with various narcotic herbal blends all tainted with lamp oil kerosene.

Gas mantles fizz luminescence while seedy booths closet clandestine confidences within rosewood panelled walls. If only the sax player had a ten bob note for every secret passed between pursed lips as he horn-honks and wails through the classics. He always wears sunglasses. They make him invisible, so he thinks. Punters speak as though he's not there on solo breaks. He reflects their lives in their own eyes. He's good. Really good at that. The notes he plays sequence conspiracies to murder, assignations and breakdowns. There is little to differentiate between any of them. He sees money and glances exchanged for various tricks, licks and reasons from the players and the fixers and the extortionists and the blackmailers and the dealers and the fences. The victims and perpetrators of vile schemes and activities face their lot. All life crawls its way along this boulevard of vice, too wrapped up in its own ego to understand where it's going wrong for each and every soul serving in this purgatory of guilt and shame. This dark ark of adulterated insanity.

A full blue moon rises tonight. A hot air balloon in size and distance shines a torch-like beam on Asylum Way. Its' inhabitants blink as they scurry along. It's the closest they get to walking out in the sun. Daylight only exists for others. For this place, the night is the only time for shadows to be seen.

The sound of the sax reverberates along the cobble-ribbled thoroughfare. There is always the hope that one day night owls and bob howlers will simply leave this pitiful place. It's the notes in bars that keep them in, telling them what to do and when. Tonight is going to be the turn of someone else to tap into their inner horrors.

See the hack from a tawdry tabloid rag those of strong desire. Notes worm their way hot into ears and finally brains, agitating the mind to a further stage in the destruction of chilled hearts.

The loner in the corner has finished his drink now and he's off to pick up that club-like cane from the stick stand by the entrance to this dive. He seeks one particular lady of the night.

The street has now become a theatre. Each doorway a promiscuous arch. Her eyes shine from that corner-shop recess. She's so petite, but carries years of streetwise nouse beyond her age. Eleanore's worked these streets for ten of her 27 years in this hell. The hack pays her service fees and they dissolve stage left.

An audience begins to gather.

Can you hear those grunts from the hack?

Eleanore screams after a sickening thud.

The audience gasps as she runs stage centre pursued by a drooling hunched-back figure carrying a blood stained club.

The sax becomes abstract and nightmarish. It's sharper and more jagged in a be-bop way.

Eleanore flashes a blade from her pocket as the hack rains further blows to her ribs.

He recoils.

As she falls to her knees she sizes up the opportunity to plunge the serrated blade into the soft underbelly of her assailant.

The space falls silent as the hack drops the club to the floor and looks down at the blade protruding from his stomach.

Blood blooms like a rose on his shirt front.

He notices that the handle to the blade was in the shape of a saxophone.

His eyes fix on Eleanore as she turns to the audience and withdraws the blade from his mortal wound.

He falls in time to the floor as jazz from the saxophonist fills the chilled night air.

Eleanore wipes blood from the slick flick blade on her underskirt and passes it to a stage hand as she exits stage right.

The audience bay for more as she takes a final curtain call.

The venue clears. It's swept and mopped in stage lit darkness.

An officer of misrule enters the street and calmly suggests there was nothing more to see and breaks up groups of stragglers and revellers.

A full moon sets to rapturous applause as all hell holes re-fill empty glasses. The saxophone strikes up, there it is. Right on time to wonder who will be the next star to fall in this theatre of release on the next wailing blue moon.

Take me to see the Punch and Judy show on the park mother. Please!

5 The Stringing Tree

The guide looks old.

Not old in years but old as from another time now lost to this world.

His face is crazed like an old map that had been wedged in a car door pocket for many miles. Sun dried, sun bleached and road worn. Some might say simply dog eared.

He brought his own angle to telling and selling the story of the newly refurbished Summerlands Park.

The guide went by the name of Mr Crowhammer. No-one knew why, except that his hair sometimes had the appearance of two crows nesting.

No-one knew where he came from, where he lived or, indeed, anything about him. The tours had become a tradition and Crowhammer a legend with tourists. Summerlands Park was an important area for visitors, both historical types and hysterical ones.

Fact or phantom? It drew them in. Tourists, ghost hunters, local historians. They all have a personal experience to witness and take home, gift wrapped. It had become a place to mean all things to all people and that was its success.

Summerlands Park had recently been rebranded. Gibbets Cross, as it had been known for centuries, now seemed an inappropriate name. The area had had money thrown at it by the local council in an attempt to upgrade amenities. All of the broken glass and litter, filth and other detritus associated with alcohol or illicit drugs had been removed. A new family area had been built. Furniture and playground equipment utilised the timber from trees that had been removed on the grounds of being a danger to the public.

One infamous tree was now supporting the swings in the playground in an attempt to promote the outdoors and natural play. A bit more community service was indeed needed for this ancient timber to flex its form.

At twilight a murder of crows would descend upon and around the swings that only earlier had been the focus of family fun and play. Even local vandals had left this place alone.

Not long after the refurbishment of Summerlands Park, a local gang flew in the face of decency and set about reclaiming the park as theirs and in so doing began destroying the hard work that had gone into making the park a safe environment. One gang member took it upon himself to set about the swings and burn them down. This was singularly the worst move he could've made.

Terrified screams were heard across the park and all the gang members assembled to watch the spectacle of the life being drawn from their gang leader by bounds of ivy winding around his rigid body and pulling him up to the top rail of the swings. Other gang members tried to help, only to be caught up in the same way. Three hanged that night. Their final dance caused the rest of the gang to disappear in all directions screaming blue murder. Three bodies were recovered the next morning. They lay on the safe play tarmac beneath the tree. The swings were untouched and, as for the victims, no marks or signs of asphyxiation were found. There was no ivy to be seen around the swings either or, indeed, any cut marks from the 'hanging'. Traces of LSD were found in the blood of the victims and the snivelling gang survivors, which only confirmed the reasoning behind the addled statements of those who witnessed the event. Their words put down to a drug-induced mass hallucination. Since that night all vandalism ceased.

Many conspiracy theories were born from this incident. Was it a psychic happening? Was there another potentially related inter-gang motive at work? One historian put together a theory that was so fantastic that it was only believed as an urban myth after it had been publicly ridiculed.

Crowhammer had focused his studies on crime and punishment in the area. He discovered from old maps that Summerlands Park sat directly over a network of ancient footpaths and, in particular, one main crossroads. To the side of this crossroads stood an ancient tree. Locally known as the Stringing Tree at Gibbets Cross, it was known to many generations. Its remoteness made it an ideal spot for murder and robbery in days gone by. Those found guilty of such crimes were hanged from the branches of the tree and left there as reminder of law and order. Their after-death fate was left to the chiselling beaks of crows. Many a ne'er do well tried to tear this tree down, as it became a symbol of law over crime, only for them to be found lifeless beneath its shadow. Death was always recorded as an open verdict.

The name of Gibbets Cross was officially changed to Summerlands Way when housing had encroached over the once remote countryside and, after local calls and demands for a safe green space, the park was defined.

Many said how safe they felt when visiting this park. As if someone watched over them, a guardian angel maybe. Many came to see the thousands of crows descend, especially on a September evening to pick the park clean of detritus before heading home.

The tree stood open limbed in welcome. Crowhammer? Well, he stood in silence next to the swings. All the people and the crows had left him to his research. A breeze pushed the swings as he took a look around. For a moment, he felt a gentle protective embrace as an ivy leaf scuttered along the pathway just a few feet away. His story told, Crowhammer disappeared into a heat haze. He would return for another tour someday soon. Well, at the very least, I would hope so.

The blue lights are here again.

Watch her, the one in stilettos. I don't like the way she looks at me.

6 Dark Eyes In The Rain

Oh she's seen many things.

Puts herself on the line.

Never gives way when she knows she's right.

Always stands by her principles.

Her judgement has not once failed her and it isn't going to start now. I can tell you.

From the outside of the building you can see her face looking out from the upstairs window that by now will be streaked with rain.

Clouds pass over her gaze like the transient storms that surround her imprisonment.

She cries on the inside.

I have seen her.

When she's sad the clouds are heavy.

When she sings the sun comes out and the birds will sing with her.

When she's tired, the moon will rise and break the clouds like a balloon sailing above the swaying trees that gather so many of her thoughts.

Sometimes moonlit dew lights the nearby well like a snail trail.

It contains her secrets and memories of past lovers you know.

She will not recall how many they total, but that's inconsequential for now.

The well is as deep as her emotions. She probably thought that a few more wouldn't hurt.

She told me that she lost her treasure to a pug-nosed runt of a man whose manners and cleanliness were as base as a farm yard.

When he took advantage he squealed like a pig in a shambles.

When he released her, he wiped the dribble from his mouth, tucking his shirt into his food-stained britches.

Dazed, she silently raised a heavy candlestick that contained the flame that only minutes earlier had cast his grotesque shadow on the wall by the window.

Within seconds she brought the makeshift weapon down with a sickening thud on the back of his porcine head. He lay bleeding like the proverbial.

His body made a resounding splash in the well water.

She promised herself that all men passing the remote house who took similar liberties would befall the same fate.

Dealing with the cadavers herself became easier once a routine was found.

No-one asked about the disappearances as she only ever portrayed innocence and ignorance.

After each murder it would rain for the whole of the day until she was reborn in dawn's first light. Her new mood would be held aloft on a thermal of naivety in salutation to the smiling sun.

Then she would sing a haunting song to still her aching heart.

Upon my true love's heart I sing.
I gave my heart and everything.

From oceans of devotions I feel for he.
And for all that he does in his love for me.

One fine Autumn day she says she was out cutting logs for the fire when a man of some means rode past. Upon hearing the song, he pulled up his horse and after dismounting, he quietly walked a little closer to find the source of such a beautiful voice.

He appeared to her like a vision.

She cried at his sensitivity and trusted him from the moment that her gaze entrapped him. He smiled and complimented her on such a fine song.

She wiped her hands and poured tea from a boiling pot that was heating on the yard fire. She always had a spare cup.

They sat around the chopping block chit-chatting as the traveller's thirst was quenched.

He was not like the others.

They would have used her by now.

He simply stood up from the makeshift table and bowed before making a move towards his horse. In desperation, she shouted to him that he couldn't leave her and that she wouldn't allow it.

Confused, he turned and saw madness in her eyes.

She asked if he found her pretty.

He said he did.

She asked if he liked her company.

He said he did.

She asked why he was leaving.

He said that he feared falling in love with her and that he could not stand her rejection.

She asked if it was love he was after or what lay beneath her clothing.

Shocked, he turned away in order to get onto his horse.

She pulled him back and with a side swipe of a hefty log, she crushed his pretty head to a bloody pulp.

She unsaddled his horse and made the beast comfortable in the stable before dragging the body back to the table where moments earlier they had chatted.

She poured him another cup of tea and her finger brushed his matted hair from over his eyes.

He did not purse his lips to take a sip.

And today she gazes from the upstairs window.

She is handcuffed and in the company of a police officer whilst the well is searched for the bodies of the guilty tormentors and the innocent handsome suitor who showed nothing but love.

He was later laid to rest, free from those dark eyes in the rain.

They are taking another one away.

7 The Killing of Fair-Face

Tremors start in her hands at around 8pm.

Strange that they take on contorted shapes then. Their shadows dance multiplied by firelight and spluttering paraffin lamps. They are as timely as a tidal change.

Her mind races.

Those sea spume stallions of nightmares are stampeding through her uneasiness casting gnarled vignettes of swirling whirlpool imagery. They eclipse candle flicker into irregular spasms for the folio that lies before her contains evils so dark that light is only a figment of imagination.

She takes a long gulch of spirit from a glass and pours another from a razor edge cut glass decanter which is already getting too close to needing a refill.

That's when it happens, without fail, time and time again.

Her face comes to mind through descending transient mists of experience.

Her lithesome body dancing in dim kerosene stage light as if her inner demons were coaxing a physical response.

Eleanore welcomes her troubled yet erotic climax and sirens the scented darkness with the call of her dark pleasures.

She could be seen smiling a smile that could freeze dry Maytime blossom. She could bring a perpetual winter to those in her company with her presence-created malevolence.

An icy chill blows before her.

I wish they'd close that door.
They always leave it open.
Would you be a dear? Thank you.

Now where was I?
Ah yes! I was here and you were there.

I recall talking to her that night in the cells before sentencing. She was unfortunately reaching a full stop.

Lamplight efficacy lay in slashed diagonals of shadow across her haunted features.

The blood, still coagulating in her hair and on her hands. It peeled away from her fingertips as she triumphantly wrung those murderous, artistic hands during confessions of her recent successes.

She had seen them.

Those two.

Him and her.

How could they?

Caught them in the act.

Maria and him.

Projecting their form upon the trellis wall from her favourite chintz bed clothes.

Their screams of defiant innocence brought her closer to her final actions.

She knew what she had seen and she used her last penny to phone for a trusted voice.

I would have been there, if only she had made me the recipient of that call.

He, however, over the years had taken her for a ride and was now breaking-in the next filly to fuel his addictions.

Eleanore told me that she could handle his gambling.

Accept the evenings of opium and absinthe, but sex with other women drove her beyond her own check mate boundaries.

She told me that her adversary was so easy to remove from her poisoned heart, as easy as giving up a bust hand at Black Jack.

Even he should be able to understand that. A simple accusatory letter to the seductress in red ink removed her from sight and into a strait-jacket. She was very persuasive and her opposition highly suggestive.

Again I hear Eleanore, her voice echoing still in the rooms of my mind.

Calm, monotonous and devoid of emotion.

She recalled loading the pistol.

One bullet at a time.

A mind's eye transmission begins to run.

She brushes dressing table face powder from the warm brass cartridges that until now she'd kept in a black lace bra next to her left breast. Sliding each lead seed of death into its fated chamber she smiles with a caressing sensuality and a lick of her pouting ruby tone lips. Their glistening veneer too thick to see through and too thin to be merciful.

She smiles at the last click of the safety catch. Its' cadence tutting through the silence of intense thought and blinding focus.

Placing the heart heavy revolver into her clutch bag, Eleanore made for the door. It took her to the corridor overburdened with chemical violet scented carpet freshener and on to the lift which wasn't working. She continued down thirteen floors and on through the foyer into the grim grasp of a rain barbed night. She checked her appearance in a doorway reflection.

Tomorrow, she thought she might treat herself to some new accessories. Make a new start. Always best to, she once told me.

Block brutalist street refractions house silicate kaleidoscopes. They portray swirling acid leaves onto a windswept Fauvist Autumn day. She passes through them, as all transients do.

Her target sits in the cafe as usual, next to the back door, as cool as the moon even though the air was thick with steaming macchiato and sickly viscous oozings of flavoured syrups. A hint of exotic leaf enters her mind through trap doors that were normally kept locked. This night was different. It bordered on the obtuse, as many words were uttered but collectively were inconsequential. The back door was significant in the set up, as this was his usual entrance. Tonight it would prove to be his exit.

He sits unperturbed by the sight of her entering the cafe. He looks out from behind his blue sky eyes that freeze in terror as pistol fire buries itself into his temple. The trigger clicking unquestioningly beneath perfectly manicured nails of his nemesis. His guilt stamped across his face as a blood red rose blooms just below his hairline, the cannoning bullet sent burning deep into the cortex of past deeds before lodging into the sticky nicotined paint of the doorframe that had stood witness behind him. Caught out, he slumped forward into the brown sugar that spilled freely on the white linen table cloth that later became his makeshift, coffee-stained shroud. She holds him in her arms after placing the murder weapon down. Raising his head, she clutches him to her bosom before positioning him for one last look into his soul. Suddenly the noise of the cafe amplified around her like an orchestra hitting a crescendo.

Waiters carried his body out through the kitchen and into the back alley.

Let's face it sights like this are bad for business.

Staff promptly changed the cutlery, offering house red to any takers. No-one saw a thing. The band changes track and strikes up, 'When you're smiling'.

Her lips raise up into the corners of her bow lipped mouth.

Police took statements. The victim's told them little of his evil nature. However, the witnesses did.

And now, in my mind's eye, Eleanore comes to me from her self-imposed fatalistic prison cell and calls for an understanding that few could find. And, from time to time, she will talk to me. Still she shows no remorse for her actions, even though she passed away by the rope of authority some hundred years back. There are times when she can't help herself when Fair Face visits her and sings 'The whole world smiles with you'.

I like the old songs do you? Hear that? It's another one on the way.

8 Midnight Ice

It's always then.

Just then.

That moment when the clown's face positions itself for the expressionist depiction of debauchery and turns to snarl like a rabid beast I hear those damned chimes.

Midnight sounds of childhood revisit me through the gas taint smell of Papa Cornetti's penny lick creamy cream whipped ices. He calls at the dead of night on the estate doors of my hidden thoughts. I am held to ransom every time by an axe-wielding teddy bear who stares unerringly through his bead glass eye.

He remains unwittingly mounted to the grinning grill of the nursery palette painted van that now hums like an angry Autumn wasp in the curved whorls of my outer limits.

The chimes continue, relentlessly swirling in my head, windblown and beckoning in their wildness.

Dum de dum de dum de dum, dum de dum de dum da.

Familiar and threatening, they beckon me trance-like to the light that radiates from the habit-forming serving hatch.

I navigate my way between night walkers stepping off kerbs in neon utterances, being simultaneously aware of car cruisers menacing the highway.

I cross safely.

There will be no blood on the streets tonight. Not mine at least.

That evening sleep was but a fingertip distance away as Papa Cornetti plied his trade to the innermost mind of insomnia.

The peel of tri-tone klaxon chimes struck chords of reaction inside my cavernous skull that was rapidly becoming a mausoleum of tainted memory.

I remember strawberry syrup always fuelled dreams of carnage.

Lime, I was told, echoes wanton waste.

I was too afraid to ask for raspberry.

Life now oozes across the white folded sheets of ice-laced experience and into the waiting waffle weave arms of finality.

'Papa Cornetti, how are you? How are your wife and children? Well, I hope?'

Papa Cornetti smiles and offers an additional flake and lime juice.

I have never risked lime before.

Should I?

Through sleep the chimes wrap themselves around my nightmares.

In and out of phase the cartoon cell slides and chases tails around the beaten panels of seaside imagery.

A magnificent magician's cane falls to the gutter side as the van leaves. I call, but the chimes drown my words into familiar nursery rhymes.

I pick up the cane.

It feels wrong.

It grips my hand to the point of breaking my fingers.

Bones click as the constriction continues and I am there in the circus parade where clown cars backfire and disintegrate at will.

I find myself on a mist swept street.

It's a little after four am.

It always is.

A dim light glimmers through the thick night air from a cottage furnace. A hammer is heard ringing on the stippy anvil within. Dum de dum de dum de da. The cane flexes and indicates that its' fate is not here and now.

We walk on to an open night-soil entry, where a drunk lies burbling indecipherably into a drain cover. He rolls onto his back and belches a stomach-churning belch tainted with acidic intoxicant.

The cane leads me round and further along the street to where prostitutes smell of lime juice and pimps ply late night bids to pox-ridden tricks. A lamplight lady whistles as I pass in the shadows and her two-for-one cohort hums dum de dum de dum de dum dum de dum de da da.

Even here I cannot resist the lead of the cane to the jeweller's window.

It glistens magpie-bright with content giving stars to night before the silicate fractures into a million shards and my pockets become heavy with contraband.

Police whistles cut the night, dum de dum de dum de da dum de dum de da da.

We run, the cane and I, to a street corner where midnight chimes echo from a more innocent time.

I ask for an ice cream from Mr Cornetti. 'How much?' I asked.

'A pocket full of gold and a fistful of stars,' he replied.

I empty my pockets and in an instant the cane and Mr Cornetti were gone.

They come and go, come and go. Then they go.
Spending too much time on that blasted computer
thing than dealing with us.

9 Techno Head

Who's there?
Is there someone there?
Just there, then. In the shadows.
In the corner of the screen.
Are you a passing eclipse of wind-tossed mind trees?
Are you real?
Phantoms before dawn?
Please make yourself known.
I see a firefly.
A point of light in infinite darkness.
I hear you.
I don't hear you.
I see you.
I don't see you.
I sense you.
You are in code.
I decipher your intentions.
Yes.
No.
On.
Off.
Light.
Dark.
Click.
Clack.
Snick.
Snack.
Flip.

Flop.
And.
Nand.
Not.
Or.
Nor.
Zero.
One.
He saw.
See saw.
Black.
White.
Shade.
No shade.
Cast.
No shadow cast.
Mood on.
Mood off.
Drone view.
Hive control.
Out of control.
Reality.
Non reality.
Omnipresent avatar.
Friend of certain insanity.

Maria is known to most as Techno Head. The only girl in the cyber cafe who liked dark chocolate sprinkles served upon the crest of a double strength cappuccino. The cafe internet interface was Victorian steampunk in style, the walls coated in heavy metal frippery and vapour residue. Whatever its appearance, the outdated equipment would ultimately be destined for a scrapyard beach in the Far East.

On cold nights winds freeze dried cobbled streets into ribbles of sheet ice. We would meet in the heat of the cafe.

We were moths drawn to ultraviolet. Waiting for a ready or not zap flash to launch us into cyberspace by simply becoming the connecting bridge across anode and cathode.

Maria was always in the corner seat with her face illuminated by terminal screen four. When her twenty minutes expired she would look up, nod to the proprietor, wink, reboot and load up.

She communicated hi and bye, but little else. Her partner sat next to her, his long hair flowing like a talcum river from beneath his stove pipe hat. His beard had age and the whole look supported the concept of wisdom. If he did have wisdom, he seldom managed to share it as he remained transfixed by the reflections in his girlfriend's eyes.

Reflections that were not his.

He would top up her coffee at regular intervals and keep her seat when nature called. On her return, she would gaze through the silicon port where she continually held vigil.

It was a strange thing that happened one evening. Her features froze as she gazed out onto the fringes of cyberspace where digital wraiths and mythical pixels dance in a technological dawn waiting for a questioning host to barb-snag their jagged edges into.

Some said they saw something enter her mind's eye. A pin prick of light piercing the furrow that laced her brow. Some reported a scimitar of indigo light slicing through her gaze and splitting the matrix of her make up.

It is believed by observers and cyber philosophers that this purely theoretical light contains all of the shadows held in the digital universe.

Maria didn't move.

No-one heard her blink.

No-one heard her breathe.

No-one heard her cry.

A stranger to the hostelry noticed the dark stain of cyberspace in her eyes and tears of binary strands welling up in the ducts that seldom held emotion.

D
DE
DEL
DELE
DELET
DELETE
DELETED

I mean how do you cry logic?

She was held in a closed loop.

Feedback without end.

A primal scream for the new age.

But what of Maria?

I peered into her world through her staring eyes, watching billions of connections being made within her mind.

Silicon horror rose inside a carbon brain, turning it black with loss of empathy.

She was endless, infinite and confined to a chair.

There was a small scar, just there, on her forehead indicating the point of entry from this demon dart.

If only I could reach out to her.

No. I mustn't.

She is crystallising in front of our eyes.

Ready to shatter like glass.

Shards.

Shards in the shape of darts, carborundum blue.

Another incursion

Another way in to an open door mind.

The last time I saw Maria she was held behind prison bars to keep her from harm and everyone else from hurt.

She wore impenetrable glasses.

No-one is allowed to look into her eyes.

She is no longer part of this world other than a stepping stone, a bridge rectifier, one step away from eternity.

Another person will sit at terminal four tomorrow.

I'm told her name is Eleanore.

Maria's ex-boyfriend will bring her coffee.

Can you hear that tolling bell?
Who is it tolling for now I wonder?

10 Church Chimes

The church on the hill stands in doom-laden gloom.

Even the earliest depictions of the site tells the same story of joyless austerity.

Many put it down to years of morally flawed incumbents representing their angry god in such an ancient spiritual space.

These self imposed representatives of the divine taught fear and penance not love and forgiveness.

The energy there dwindled over the years. Too many takers and not enough givers. It became a mere building to share priestly gossip through the ears and mouths of faith holders, rumour mongers and hypocrites.

Trees had been torn down to make way for this unhappy dysfunctional man-made bauble to place on the crown of thorns.

An arboreal cathedral stood there once.

A joyous broadleaf grove of ancient spirits once guarded the landscape. It was human greed and the axe that reduced everything to scrubland bed rock. The foundations today contain within its fortress-like walls the imprisoned dead whilst keeping the living out. It makes no difference how many crosses speak of lives long since gone. They give no redemption to lead hypocrites.

The walls are dour due to the impregnation of two centuries of industrial grime. Inside tells another story. Walls running damp but brass and gold shine brightly in candle lit splendour.

Spires aspire to reach heaven's lofty heights, but serve only to impede the view. Its' hourly bell tower boom was filled with a sanctuary of dread. It cracked the sky like an eggshell with a hammer blow as heavy as Thor.

A dutiful congregation shuffled through the doors of chastity. There were no smiles or welcomes. The nave was mildewed and cold and the only comfort given was from sputtering tallow. Smoke burrowed into the eyes and lungs of the loyal and the sermons were long, prying and accusatory, as if a spotlight had fallen on the innocent to question them until a weft of guilt was found. As for the guilty, well, they washed their spiritual hands in the sanctity of wealth and politics.

One such awakening led to an incident that many have tried to forget. Otis was a pig farmer. A simple straight forward pig farmer. He had no complications about him in life or psyche. He was devout in his faith and committed to his work. Up to sixteen hours a day he tended his livestock from birth to market. Livestock auctions and the sale of farm produce took place on the last Friday of the month then. August had been a hot one and the walk to market was dry and dusty. Otis tried to keep his two pigs in scant shade as much as possible to keep them cool and comfortable.

Close by he heard the screams of a lady. He tethered the pigs under a tree and went to find the source of distress. He recognised the squire's son, a serial confessionist wrestling seamstress Eleanore to the ground. Her clothes already torn, she fought blindly to save herself from the motives and questionable morals of this man. Eleanore was often seen walking to market in her best clothes and had caught the eye of Otis many times. Otis' feelings of love for her were often the subject of many a whisper at the church on the hill. As Eleanore lay motionless and punched unconscious. Otis set about the squire's son, who saw he was no match for Otis and so ran away like only a coward would.

Otis knelt by Eleanore's side and stroked her hair away from her closed eyes. He straightened her clothes and made her decent again. How he loved her.

Suddenly Eleanore's eyes opened and she began to fight off Otis. He saw her expression of horror, meant for someone else. She screeched a primal scream of survival just as others on their way to market came to find out more about the commotion. They saw Otis holding back the flailing arms of Eleanore, telling her to be quiet and that it was ok. A circumstantial moment that led to such a miscarriage of justice.

Otis was arrested, his pigs taken back to the soon-to-be-ruined farm which the squire's son acquired at a below market price due to a skewed moral and media association. The squire gave a tied cottage to Eleanore's family to help ease the pain of such an abhorrent attack on one so fragile and pure.

Otis went to the gibbet tree at the crossroads and danced away at sunset to the tune of seven winds in its branches and inevitably to the sound of those damning church bells.

Eleanore gave birth to a son nine months later. He was the spitting image of his father.

What time is it? Nearly past. Thank you.

11 Laser Ball

Drones filled polluted skies above that self inflicted metropolis of Precinct 13.

Police state regulations were well in control even then.

Huge swathes of Angerland became no-go areas after the fifty year old 'Isolate to Accumulate' deals of 2020. The only thing the state had left was to sell tumbledown tower blocks for prison space annexations. The deal was bailed out by an iron fist government that set out to imprison decent law-abiding people in poverty and so by entrapping them all within the incarceration boundaries of State lines. Blue identity cards had to be carried at all times to cross without favour border controls. The only way forward it seemed was to either sign up to the state or find underground revolutionary movements to gain safety in number survival.

Curfew began religiously at 20.00 hours, just in time for Media Corps to start its propaganda reports on how well the government was working for everyone. It ruled by fear and ignorance, and allowed the worst criminal elements to roam freely within cordoned-off areas of the capital. These places were called Red Zones and no-one could enter them for fear of death and a locally endorsed hefty fine, in some cases both and in that order.

Street-side TVs would spring into life, volumes full to ear splitting were cranked up just in case you didn't choose to hear the glorification of state. The droning words of criminal intake and successes of correction methods reverberate through urban landscapes that cover pretty much all of the once green fields of Angerland.

Permissible areas Green Zone drones were launched at 20.15 hours. Public Order Drones, or POD's, were launched at 20.30 hours. They originally set out to protect the public, but now they only sought to incriminate it. Anyone breaking the curfew would be immediately arrested and sent to an Amber Zone, effectively, a pre-trial hell hole of isolation.

Trade in false passports and sick notes from mother were the grey market economy here, alongside drug trafficking, slave labour and prostitution. Prison intake is free market stake holder profit. Opposition politics was banned and anyone found to be talking against the aims of government are put under house arrest.

Much of the anti-government propaganda was hidden in poems and songs and carried a coded system of words that meant something to those in the know. Live music and spoken word events were allowed. They were mainly singalongs to the joys of battle but everything is treated with suspicion by the police. Events were monitored by CEDs, or Community Engagement Drones, where public performance content could be recorded and analysed on the grounds of the Trumpentine 'wholesomeness' mandate from 2020. In fact, Angerland was mooted to become the latest star on the Stars and Bars.

I digress.

A new drone had recently been brought into service by yet another police department initiative called Next Wave. This police department have the power to stop, seize and scan anyone or anything. It contains a new weapon: the Laser Ball. It was the first drone to carry a potentially lethal weapon. Some earlier models carried TASERs.

Indiscriminate policing has led to several deaths with the overuse of this facility. Some officers clearly sought fun and pleasure by using this type of law enforcement from the comfort of an armchair in a CCTV control room.

I heard the other day that the Meet For Freedom Lobby had just broken from its scheduled meeting. Its secret hideaway is only ever known an hour before the gathering. It's changed for each meeting, but trust is difficult within the group as the police department is always ready to infiltrate at the earliest opportunity. Members are seen as enemies of home rule and after any meeting those gathered were told to leave in ones or twos to avoid detection. They had to be instructed to stick to the shadows after curfew. Drones can only sense movement. Their eyes remain somewhat poor in the dark. It is thought that mistaken identity could be used as a means of defence by the authority if statistics were below target.

Numbers at the meetings have risen steadily. This is a major boost to a renegade party but it's also brought division within the collective. Some advocate the use of violence to provide a safe haven in which to live. Others see this as counterproductive and that peaceful measures of politeness and diplomacy would win the day. That was until last night.

A man, thought to be a saxophonist, sought freedom. He was fed up with being told what to think, what to do and when to do it, and so decided to go out on the corridors after curfew to wave the flag of liberty. Two drones immediately detected his advances on the precinct. Hands and eyes controlled focus and distance for part facial recognition. The screens rolled a banner, which said 'Freedom Fighter - Enemy of Law - Laser Ball deployed.'

The man jeered at the drones as they encircled him. He waved his flag and sang songs of freedom. The officers in the control room sipped coffee and smiled as the Laser Ball drone positioned itself alongside the other drones. For a moment, everything fell silent. With a flash of intense light a plasma ball was released and, within a split second, that poor man's body fell lifeless to the floor. Officers smiled and congratulated themselves on a job well done. The drones continued with their observations. A body was found the next day by a Lobby member. The flag was still in his hands. He had a hole the size of a pea bored straight through his brain. Revolution by any means was the only way to find freedom. The time to talk was over.

Are you still here? Please go away.

12 Wandering Between Worlds

That mock Rococo mirror sees everything in silent reflections you know.

It's fixed in silent judgement from a vantage point above the mantle shelf.

Occasionally we find the mirror tilting one way or another. It has seen many people come and go I suppose, each sharing their own brand of vanity with varying degrees of pleasure or disgust over the years.

Within its silvered veneer it records everything. It's creating a composite world of all those who collectively share in its flattery. The fresh face of youth to the decay of age, it holds them all. A cosmic repository of transience.

They say the mirror began its life over a century or so ago. It has seen fashions come and go. It sees what lies beneath the costume, observing skin and bone and even the bio chemistry of each individual presenting themselves. It stamps their DNA with full stops, building up agony and ecstasy in equal measures. It is an X-ray, x-rated voyeur given permission to invade innermost secrets laid bare by the pouting and the preening, the elderly and the weaning.

Maria wishes that she is more like her reflection, as she arches her back in a peak of ecstasy. She glances up from sweat-stained sheets as the heat of the day intensifies her wantonness. She holds his image in her mind's eye managing a look towards herself as she lies in resultant panting from self indulged pleasure.

He would not be back anytime soon.

Her stars had placed exo planet Pluto in conjunction with full phase Venus, and Scorpio was rising. It spelled out danger. There was no time for romance. It was all transformational. Sex, death and rebirth and she was driven by them all. No more was she to be the slave nor the skivvy. Now it was her time and she was taking it. If only she believed more when it comes to the final act of freedom.

She dreams that her fingers are someone else's. She fantasises that the lips at her breasts belong to the object of her daily desire. She rolls and ripples in an onrush wave breaking against the salty crags of her darkest desires. She can hold her release no longer.

She notes her climb down and becomes self conscious. She becomes a photograph in a gilt edged frame. She is the bust of a Greek goddess, a subconscious lover witnessing the unburdening of her taut lines and sinews. Her sweat gathers as shoreline rock pools do in the pits of serpentine form. Her body glistens like hoar frost in a full moon.

Her breathing subsides into a gentle tidal breath rising and falling in rhythmic time with the undulations of her physicality that has reached its zenith and has stretched her to the limits of ecstasy.

She drifts mindside. A sense of weightlessness overcomes her and places her in the arms of afterglow.

Through her apartment windows she lies in sunlit glades, summer caresses her skin. She feels the moss and grass beneath her and, for once, experiences a universal connection with another world. A place where she finds true fulfilment and happiness away from reality. Away from her tormentors.

If she had lost her way, at least now she has found her destination. See her claw at the twisted bed clothes as another wave peaks and drenches her in satisfaction. Her demons still wait in the shadows, waiting for a quiet time to embark on hunting their prey. She knows they are there. They are always there huddled in a forgotten recess of her rampaging mind. He had seen to that. Her last lover had taken her to the outer limits of paranoia. He was a grand master at mind games. He dished out pleasure for double the pain. She allows her eyes to half open. He is still sitting there, pupils dilated, with a glassy expression. She closes her eyes again and finds herself on a stage. A chanteuse emotionally naked to the gas lights. She is attired in a green evening dress and begins to sing of love and deceit accompanied by jealousy.

No-one can take my man, my man away from me
And if they try then just wait and see
What instinctive wrath would befall the same
And they would relive their actions again
and again and AGAIN!

The band finishes after the obligatory saxophone solo and she opens her eyes to look towards the mirror. She is lying on the floor. A gun shot wound to her racing heart leaches blood neatly congealed into the form of a black rose petal motif.

She looks back to him.

Sees the knife in his throat that had choked his last laugh.

She hears sirens or maybe an ice cream van heralding an interval in proceedings?

She closes her eyes once more for a scene change, continues wandering between worlds as a dog howls from the street below and a neighbour plays late night jazz on a wind-up gramophone and look! See how the mirror smiles.

She's ever so pleasant. She always tells me that I'm a nice old man really.

13 How Long In Years

Maria had a lot to look forward to. She always broke the rules. She was once the apple of someone's eye and always a dutiful servant. Another click, another second sacrificed and sentenced to the past by the mantle clock. You know it's the main spring that drives the balance wheel past another dog tooth and on the escapement of that fate-recording timepiece don't you?

The intravenous lines gave her life and her future gave her hope, but the doctors said it was all just a question of time.

In her dreams he steered the stolen car along the alleyways. She remembered his fair face frozen in time behind the shattered windshield. She had no care, not even for herself. But there she remained, framed in the windscreen and as large as life. Another street victim of hit and run violence.

She suddenly remembered three balloons from her childhood. They were as big as harvest moons that drifted above her head. She held the tether strings tightly so as not to lose them. Mom and dad had taken her to the fair. The Hall Of Mirrors gave her distorted vision and the ice cream van played chimes in her head. A procession of candy coloured ices carouselled in her mind, with the prices of childhood attached to them and all overwritten in blue biro.

She recalled that nothing stayed the same.

Then there were the three faces that observed her from the foot of the bed. The three graces, and all the races that she had run in her life that had led her here to this point in time and vision. She was maid, mother and would be crone. That car would not take that away. She was sure of that.

Inside her head, she walked into a small room and waited outside in the corridor of a moment, waiting to be seen by fate itself. A clock face with pointing fingers directed time like a dutiful traffic cop. Which way now? She had taken another number from the ticket machine of life. It was the same each time. There was no jumping the queue. Just like waiting at a supermarket deli counter, she thought. A half pound of cheese and a sausage roll, please. Oh, and a party pack of vegetable samosas. Lamb always reminded her of slaughter.

'Customer number 11, please' crackled the tannoy.

She thought about her number. The one, the one path, the one she formed the trinity with on the hill.

How long would she have to wait in this sleep that had frozen her body but not her mind? How would she get that first message out to the world?

What would be the first thing she would taste?

The number 12 flickered and, for a moment, the screen went blank. Come in number thirteen. Is your time really up? She thought aloud. A distant sunrise headed the terminator towards her. It gathered speed as it grew broader and brighter. Her eyelids flickered open and she saw the old world with new eyes. She heard a friendly voice she instantly recognised as her daughter. Her mother stood alongside the police officer ready for a witness statement about the stolen car that took her, flicked her over and left her for dead in the gutters of her mind.

The car was black, she muttered. High gloss, high powered and did I mention coffin black like a beetle back of painted shellac? Polished like a mirror. She heard the dull thud as metal hit flesh and bone before the silence befell her. She recalled their faces. The driver had been found murdered in a motel room. What of his accomplice? The car was found in the next state. It was out of fuel, its' nuclear engine deplete of rads. A female corpse sat lifelessly gripping the wheel. Her eyes had been removed by crows who cawed in sheer pleasure. Maria wrote in her diary on the first day of recovery, 'Remember me?' before staring at a tree in full leaf just outside her window. She looked in the mirror and knew.

Have you ever seen fate look back at you?

Someone I knew once saw their truth in its eyes.

14 Identity Crisis

Each time he reflected upon his life he saw her. A transformation emerging before his eyes.

She is kohl pencil dark-eyed and forever waiting in the frame to seduce his thoughts and beckon his soul towards a new found truth.

From where he stood, one half of the room represented his past, the other his future and he walks the line between them. A space betwixt an oak wardrobe and full length mirror is where *she* tirelessly waits. He looks again and sees that her mood today is most definitely sultry.

She is a steamy socialite ready to take on the world and beat it at every opportunity. Other times however, she could be an aesthetic butterfly waiting to flit to the next brightly-coloured flower of attraction.

On the table is a bottle of whiskey, a half crushed packet of cigarettes and a blister strip of painkillers. On the other side of the room stands a jug of filtered water, both sides poles apart, yet, both appear comfortable in each other's company. Dualities continue to swirl around him in whirlpools of anguish and desire. He smooths his jeans as she runs her long, slender fingers down her shapely legs adjusting her stocking tops to sexual perfection.

He straightens his t-shirt as she lifts her breasts into the cups of a lace edged bra and adjusts the straps to form the perfect shape.

He ties the laces on his trainers as she slips on six inch stilettos that were built for the bedroom and not the pavement.

He looks at her and she smiles a knowing smile.

He leaves for the town and she won't be back for a few hours.

Each shop window he walks past she stares back pouting her cherry bow lips in air kiss frenzies. He wonders if his mirror at home is empty. Part of him didn't want to know.

He sits in a coffee shop and she stares back from the waves of his skinny latte. How could he ever be free from her obsession with him and his with hers?

He goes back to his flat and looks towards the mirror. She stands there smouldering with intent. He undresses. She is undressed. She stands there in fishnets and a basque.

She slowly removes them to stand naked before him. Her breasts perfectly sculptured. Their hands meet at their individual points of pleasure. Minds race, thoughts collide, deepest desires overflow in an arcing rainbow of release after the storm.

Still breathless guilt engulfs heated moments. He puts on his new shirt and trousers. She puts on a blouse and jeans and ponytails her long hair. He sits in the chair and she goes into the reflected image of the kitchen. It seems that their roles are now clearly defined. He is certain that any move on his part would take the relationship even further.

He pours a whiskey over rocks and sips it slowly. The temptation is always to take it down in one but that often leads to a binge session to blot her memory out. Even in sleep she is there, waiting and endorsing his innermost fears and revelations. Nothing could erase her from his mind. He wants to embrace her and love her even more each time their intimacy engulfs them.

He had had other relationships, though these were no more than a series of shallow tableaux ending with closed curtains of lies and deceit at the epilogue, but somehow he feels that this relationship is right.

Standing up he walks towards the mirror, reaches out to touch the glass. She does the same. Their arms intertwine through the silvered finish. Their eyes fix on each other as she steps through the glass and into his arms before disappearing from sight. For a moment, there is no reflection and no room. Everything falls silent. He looks again towards the mirror and sees himself for the first time. He is the sultry vixen. He is the homely casual dresser. They are all one and the same to him. He cries at the revelation. He puts on his make up and pulls on a dress, straightens it with a bend of the knees and an arch of the back. He lifts his breasts into the cups of his bra and slips on the stilettos and smiles. The reflection reappears and she smiles back at herself. The room is different. No division, all one. She knows she is at home and she looks again and sees his smile. She is now complete. She pours herself a drink from the filter jug and goes back for a second look in the mirror. He only sees a true reflection and winks.

Thanks for coming to see me. I enjoy our chats.

15 Falling To Earth

This old man with feather-like hair has seen it all by standing at his end of the street. Memories run along the pavements of his mind's eye as he darts along the alleyways of childhood, riding that old bike, noting where life has taken him. Door to door, house to house and bar to bar.

The houses still look the same but the atmosphere has changed. There are no factory smog palls nor chemical smells anymore. The cemetery ice cream van is parked up. The driver asleep at the wheel. The serving hatch has a sign that reads 'closed to whenever'.

Eleanore no longer lives at number 20 neither does Maria live at the junction with Cross Street. All the old families have moved out to be systematically replaced by selfish unseeing fish who close curtains and lock doors and keep everything out. He is out of his time.

A car screeches to a halt outside the bank. The driver, a hoodie, pries the front off the cash machine with a well-worn jemmy, helping themselves to instant free cash before driving off at high speed. No-one would catch them, as no-one was left to chase them following the policing revolution of low intervention.

Budget cuts have downed the drones and the only true free market exists with permanent vacancies.

Local economy led clip joint casinos and strip clubs into dependency creatives where shirts and dignity are lost at the spin of a wheel and a croupier's dexterity.

Forests of sale boards and broken windows greet the traveller as houses sleep in a dark unease like convicted murderers waiting for dawn to rid them of life from the end of a rope or corporate chain.

Old familiars call out from behind the imprisonment of security grilles. The old man still hears their voices, some comforting, others not so. The old soldier's wife suddenly calls out on the anniversary of an enemy strike. She remembers how it took him, her husband, away from their happiness.

The swings in the park at the back of the terrace swing like pendulums, propelled by unseen hands and leg kicks to the sky and back.

He sees the faces in windows as he walks along the street to his old address. He finds faded scratch marks on the post that once measured his height in imperial increments like the rings on trees that once stood erect and welcoming. Their stumps now left to rot by overly judicious authority cuts.

The old dance hall on the corner, where many a romance once blossomed, now seems tawdry. Its new name lit stridently by LEDs replaces the old neon illuminated one. 'Girls Like Us' was now chased above the door frame, drawing the eye away from the extortionate entry fee.

Billy Smith's Social Dance Band is lost to strict time. He found that new dances were not conducive to romantic contact with dream lovers. They are all strobe-lit gyrations offering close-contact live sexual intimacies.

Outside the club a saxophonist stands playing for hat money hunched and alone on the street. He has just played his last solo and places his brassware against the left-hand door post of the club. Lighting a cheroot he exhales and spits into the early morning air that seems fresh to his night time lungs.

Life has become cheap.

It is rumoured that another body will be found tonight, just over there where the pavement appears rusty with blood. Probably just another libertine.

A breeze picks up along the street only to blow through the soul of the old man. He looks to his gnarled hands that have turned back the years to good times and his bones feel youthful once more.

He realises that he was not long for this place.

A blinding flash of light sears across his skies, he calls out a final goodbye and is lifted high into the air.

A dog is barking at the end of the street and the old man exits his world into the waiting arms of the next.

That beautiful blue light is here again.

I really must be going. Eleanore, is that you? Oh, please tell me how is Maria?

Roses can be really beautiful at this time of year.

About Brendan Hawthorne

Poet, playwright, singer-songwriter, author and comic compère, Brendan Hawthorne is a born and bred Black Countryman. He is widely published, has held several writing residences and delivered many bespoke commissions throughout his career. He was on of Anthony Gormley's 'Fourth Plinthers' where he performed his work in Trafalgar Square, London, atop the empty plinth. Brendan was made Wednesbury Poet Laureate in 2014, appeared on BBC The One Show with Shirley Bassey and held the 'Bill o Bowes' national aware for best written dialect two years running and again in 2023. He has featured on Radio Three as an essayist and is currently working on producing his own on-line show. His recent collection of poetry *Seventies Child and Other Fashion Trends* is available via Dream Well Writing (a dyslexia friendly publication) and his latest self-published work *Calling Out Time* is available from Brendan's website www.brendanhawthorne.org.

About Jason Fullwood

Jason Fullwood also known as JLF is a freelance mixed media artist and illustrator. JLF has collaborated with Brendan Hawthorne previously in 2012 for their Mystical Menagerie project. Other accolades from JLF include featured artist in the Wolverhampton Literature festival, featured artist spotlight for HOPE VR Spaces, a former artist in residence for the National Trust's Wightwick Manor, a former studio manager of WV1 Studio and published by Immanion Press.

In addition to this JLF has also had exhibitions including Digbeth's Art Space, London's D&D New Blood Festival, Kidderminster's Boars Head Gallery, Wolverhampton's Lighthouse Media Centre, and Newhampton's Art Centre to name but a few.

Social media and Etsy links for JLF:

https://www.etsy.com/uk/shop/XJLFX

https://www.facebook.com/JaayElEf/

https://www.instagram.com/ j l f /

Printed in Great Britain
by Amazon

46702617R00057